BE REAL IN A

THE BEAUTIFUL

DARE TO BE DIFFERENT
I WANT TO MAKE AN IMPACT
WHY FIT IN WHEN YOU WERE BORN TO STAND OUT?
NO ONE IS ALL BAD

YOU WERE BORN AN ORIGINAL
YOU DON'T SEE THE REAL ME
I HIDE BEHIND HEAR ME **ROAR**
ENCOURAGE **THE** CURIOUS **KEEP** TRYING BEAUTY COMES IN ALL SHAPES **AND SIZES**

GOOD **VIBES ONLY**
RULES ARE MEANT TO BE BROKEN CREATE YOUR OWN DESTINY
BITE BACK BEAUTY BEGINS **THE** MOMENT **YOU** DECIDE TO BE YOURSELF

REBELLIOUS **SPIRITS IGNITE** REVOLUTIONS THE TRUTH IS COMPLICATED
BE THE CHANGE **YOU** WISH TO SEE IN THE WORLD
BE YOURSELF AN ORIGINAL IS ALWAYS **WORTH MORE THAN A COPY** A LITTLE REBELLION NOW AND THEN IS A GOOD CHANGE THING YOU

BE YOURSELF EVERYONE ELSE IS TAKEN
BE ORIGINAL **YOU** WERE BORN AN ORIGINAL
SPEAK OUT I SEE **THE** BEAUTY IN OTHERS IF IT DOESN'T CHALLENGE **YOU** IT WON'T CHANGE

NEVER DOUBT YOURSELF
NOBODY IS PERFECT FOLLOW **YOUR** DREAMS **TAKE THE RISK** IF YOU **CAN** DREAM IT YOU **CAN DO IT YOU ARE** ENOUGH

IT'S OKAY **NOT** TO BE **OKAY** BELIEVE IT AND ACHIEVE IT
THIS GIVE **IS** ME **ME** TRUTH **NEVER GIVE UP** BE TRUE TO YOURSELF

BE BRAVE DREAM BIG YOUR OPINION MATTERS **DREAM** CREATE INSPIRE WHAT IS **YOUR TRUTH? MAKE US** UNDERSTAND THE TRUTH MATTERS EXPRESS YOURSELF

FUTURE ECHOES

Edited By Lynsey Evans

First published in Great Britain in 2025 by:

Young Writers
Remus House
Coltsfoot Drive
Peterborough
PE2 9BF
Telephone: 01733 890066
Website: www.youngwriters.co.uk

Foreword

Since 1991, here at Young Writers we have celebrated the awesome power of creative writing, especially in young adults where it can serve as a vital method of expressing their emotions and views about the world around them. In every poem we see the effort and thought that each student published in this book has put into their work and by creating this anthology we hope to encourage them further with the ultimate goal of sparking a life-long love of writing.

Our latest competition for secondary school students, The Beautiful Truth, asked young writers to consider what their truth is, what's important to them, and how to express that using the power of words. We wanted to give them a voice, the chance to express themselves freely and honestly, something which is so important for these young adults to feel confident and listened to. They could give an opinion, highlight an issue, consider a dilemma, impart advice or simply write about something they love. There were no restrictions on style or subject so you will find an anthology brimming with a variety of poetic styles and topics. We hope you find it as absorbing as we have.

We encourage young writers to express themselves and address subjects that matter to them, which sometimes means writing about sensitive or contentious topics. If you have been affected by any issues raised in this book, details on where to find help can be found at **www.youngwriters.co.uk/info/other/contact-lines**

Contents

Court Fields School, Wellington

Erin (11)	47

Culford School, Culford

Oluwadamilola Adekeye (17)	49

Frome College, Frome

Rosie Carter (14)	52
Louie Nicholls (13)	53

Heathside School, Weybridge

Micaela Constantino (12)	54

Highfields School, Penn

Kathryn King (12)	58

ISCA Academy, Exeter

Cain Brady (12)	59

Joseph Leckie Academy, Walsall

Raheece Alikhan (13)	60

Long Field Spencer Academy, Melton Mowbray

Marcel Klause (12)	61
Layla Addesso-Arthur (12)	62
Isabella O'Flaherty	64

Looe Community Academy, East Looe

Kanisha Valentine (12)	66

North Herts ESC, Letchworth

Connor Pile (15)	67

Oakwood Specialist College, Yate

Zubaydah Hassan	68

Poole High School, Poole

Nathan Ford (12)	69
Amelie Silveira (12)	70
George Christou (12)	71
Caspar Dade (13)	72
Elisha Reid (13)	73

Regents Park Community College, Regents Park

Aiden Platt (15)	74

Seaham High School, Seaham

Tamaraseri Andrea Brisihe (11)	75

Sir John Hunt Community Sports College, Whitleigh

H Belton (13)	76

Solway Community Technology College, Silloth

Spencer Kerr (13)	77
Mimi Morgan (11)	78
Tammy Morris Crawford (13)	79
Bradley Baxter (11)	80
Bridget Irwin (13)	81
Leah Emmerson (11)	82
Maisie Emmerson (13)	83
Maisie Stalker (11)	84

Spalding Grammar School, Spalding

Charlie Edge (14)	85
Ayaan Asim-Ellahi (11)	86
Maximilian Kolodziejczyk (13)	87

St Ambrose Barlow RC High School, Wardley

Kirsty Pone (14)	88

St Andrew's CE High School, Worthing

Freya Duggan (12)	89
Frankie Morris (12)	90
Niamh Francis (12)	91
Poppy Logsdon (13)	92
Sophie Ayrey (13)	93
Carys Booth (13)	94
Alex Hatton (12)	95
Poppy McConnell (13)	96

St Bees School, St Bees

Ellie Quinn (17)	97

St Ives School, Higher Tregenna

Oscar Robinson (11)	98
Kade Mountain (12)	99
Alana Harding (11)	100

St John Baptist CIW High School, Aberdare

Jessica Shellard (11)	101
Liam Carter (12)	102
Chloe Williams (13)	104
Teddy Cresswell (12)	105
Elsie Patterson (13)	106

St Patrick's Catholic College, Thornaby

Mojola Olayode (12)	107
Amy Verrill (12)	108
Alex Bryan (12)	109
Peniel Agbanyim (13)	110
Elena Dew (12)	111
James Hannah (13)	112

Sophie Russell (11)	113
Noah Burwood-Conroy (11)	114
Janet David (12)	115
Mia Thompson (12)	116
Luke Hill (13)	117
Theo Reed (11)	118
Emily Ions (12)	119
Sam Brown (12)	120
Ava Matthews (12)	121
Cailan Wilberforce (12)	122
Faye Horner (11)	123
Isaac Woodgate (13)	124
Luke Forsyth (13)	125
Sonny Matthews (11)	126

St Thomas More High School, Westcliff-On-Sea

Alexander Martin (11)	127
Ethan Newson (11)	128
Zane Noubayo (11)	129
Kristupas Margenis (11)	130
Ogie Odigie (11)	131
Somtochukwu Ofomata-Aghaenu (11)	132
Kacper Nawrocki (11)	133

The Duston School, Duston

Acacia Carys Bisssue (15)	134
Patsy Nutt (12)	135
Nathaniel Harris (14)	136
Jake Kitching (12)	137
James Moore (15)	138
Ismail Njie (12)	139
Mason Phillips (12)	140
Coleton Vickery (11)	141
Mark Aning (14)	142

The Excelsior Academy, London

Riley Davies (13)	143
Tanzil Hossain (11)	144
Laura Krysa (13)	145

THE POEMS

BELIEVE!

FREEDOM

HONESTY

TRUTH

Nature

Nature isn't beauty
So don't tell me
We should look after it
We should care for it
We should respect it
Instead
Reject out responsibilities
We can't
Learn from nature
We should
Ignore the privilege of life
Take harmony for granted and
Forget the Earth's delights
We can never
Look at nature as though it is alive
We should
Tarnish our planet
We can't
Live with nature
Love nature or
Thrive with nature
We cannot co-exist with nature
Don't be so stupid to think
We are one with nature

(Read from top to bottom and bottom to top)

Isobel Bierton (12)

The Difference In People

Some can be round, some can be straight,
Some can be brown, some can be light,
But we are all the same in different ways,
And different lives and different homes,
We are all different, so don't judge,
We are human too, so don't judge,
If you wanna be yourself, just be it,
You are the one who loves to dance,
Be yourself, you are the best,
Fight your way for your freedom,
Love yourself, love your home,
Because you can pick your friends but not your family,
Don't be mean because that can be the last words you say to them,
Your family is your world,
Don't take advantage, they've got your back.

Lexi Wilbourne

Cherry Blossom

A haiku

Blossom time's begun,
Pink petals fall to the ground,
New season has come.

Max Patton

Inspiration

I'm grateful for the chance I've found,
To stand my ground, to prove,
It feels so good to be right here,
With nothing left to lose.

I strive to be both pure and strong,
Success my guiding star,
I love to learn, to grow each day,
And reach beyond, afar.

I won't let chances slip away,
I'll rise, I'll push, I'll fight,
For all I do, I do with love,
To make my parents bright.

They raised me up with endless care,
Their love, a boundless sea,
No debt could ever match their gifts,
Their faith has carried me.

And teachers too, they light the path,
Their wisdom helps us soar,
Without their guidance, hearts and minds
Would wander, lost, unsure.

So never let an opening pass,
Seize it, bold and free,
Believe in all the strength you hold,
You're more than you can see.

And through it all, speak only truth,
No matter what the cost,
For in the end, integrity
Is never, ever lost.

Sumayyah Khan (11)
Al-Madani Girls' School, Slough

Happy Friends

We all have a friend who is as happy as can be,
They always brighten our day for you and me.
But there is something more sinister happening beneath,
Hiding between the gaps of their great smiling teeth.
They are going through a different type of pain,
The type of pain people ignore to make them believe they're not going insane.
So she disguises herself in a happy mask for the sake of others,
It's not like anything would change, so why bother?
What can she do? If she tells her friends,
They'll try to make things mend, and in the end, nothing will change.
She runs and runs to escape the lies chasing her,
And she knows telling the truth would hurt, but she has no choice.
And sometimes she thinks if she had just told the truth,
Could she have avoided all this?

Asmaa Naveed (13)
Al-Madani Girls' School, Slough

Believe

I believe that you can achieve
Anything with the perfect mindset
Without any of the sorrowful cries, screams
And without any fret.

Life is short, quick and snappy
Live life to its fullest
Dreams, emotions, reality.

Be the one who makes a difference
Stand out from the crowd
Think outside the box
All it takes is one bubble of a thought, an idea.

Dream
Leap from your feet
If you believe,
You can achieve
You'll be able to weave
Through life's ups and downs.

Razan Rahma Dahmani (12)
Al-Madani Girls' School, Slough

My Dreams

In my dreams, the world is free
There is no war, only peace
No more orphaned children
This I hope is the end

In my dreams, there is no hunger
No people outside in the thunder
We feel sorry for them yet do nothing
This I hope is the ending

In my dreams, no one is sad
No one cries, no one is mad
People love each other, they don't hate
Just because of their race

In my dreams, we are all equal
No one with more power or money
This, I hope, is the sequel
To our story.

Aaminah Munir (13)
Al-Madani Girls' School, Slough

The Truth About Humanity

Many people think humanity is rubbish
But they are wrong
Humanity is beautiful

Life is amazingly cool
You don't have it for long
So don't become a fool

It's your life
Make it unforgettable
Make it how you want it
Don't close the door!

Humanity might feel hard
From time to time
But your light will soon
Shine!

Amna Haider (11)
Al-Madani Girls' School, Slough

Coins Are Two-Faced

Coins are two-faced, just like some people in this world.
They have a loving side
And a side you don't really want to know.
They will stab you in the back when the time is right,
Beware the coins, they will strike.
They can change their face whenever they like,
Beware the coins, they will strike.

Aisha Hakimi (13)
Al-Madani Girls' School, Slough

The Hidden Truth

D isguises are hidden
I try to keep my life private
S adness, emptiness, minds
G rey, dark worlds
U nloyal people in life
I ndependent is the best thing
S miles are disguises, which are hidden
E ven if people smile, you don't know their private life.

Zara Imran (13)

Al-Madani Girls' School, Slough

11

The Thing I Care About

The thing I care about is being me
Not having to be
Someone who is fake
So for your sake
Stop being someone you're not
The truth is really good
All your childhood
You have not been yourself
Even if that means pretending to have lots of wealth
The thing I care about is being me.

Sahar Khan (13)
Al-Madani Girls' School, Slough

Snakes

Snakes come in different shapes and sizes
Snakes are dangerous to be close with
Snakes stab you at any time
Snakes only care about themselves
Snakes are dangerous
Snakes are *not* friendly
Snakes are *fake*
It's the beautiful truth.

Fatima Bilal (12)
Al-Madani Girls' School, Slough

The World Needs To Change

Haiku poetry

Whispers of the Earth,
Silent cries for change resound,
Time to heal and grow.

Rivers murmur hope,
Mountains echo ancient dreams,
Nature calls us home.

Winds of change will blow,
Hearts united, stand as one,
Build a brighter dawn.

Falisha Noor Raheel (12)
Al-Madani Girls' School, Slough

'Who' Is You

Who decides:
Who decides what's good or bad?
Who decides who can or can't?
Who decides what is beautiful or not?
The person who decides is you.
You decide what's good or bad,
You decide who can or can't,
You decide what is beautiful or not,
You and your thoughts decide everything.
Yet still people believe they can't,
They still believe they're not enough,
They still believe they're not beautiful,
Drop the doubt, remember your beautiful truth.
Your beautiful truth is yours to take,
You are worth it,
You are strong,
You can.
The beautiful truth is you,
The person you are.

Charlotte Notman (12)

All Saints CE Academy, Ingleby Barwick

Fitting In But Losing Everything That Matters

Same hair
Same clothes
Same makeup
Same style
Same person
All to fit in
All to be noticed
Never to be you
Once discovered
Who you truly are
One by one
Destroyed
Forgotten
Lost
Comments shared about you being you
The real you
The you who can be yourself
More of an opinion
An opinion that you feel
Not everyone else
A say, a voice
Which now cannot be heard
Crowds of people overwhelm you
You try to escape
No air, no way out

Regrets build which you hoped wouldn't come
What has the world come to?
One where differences matter
Where to be normal
You have to look the same as everyone
Be you and don't change it for anyone
No matter what
You will try to fit
But build yourself in a way
That works for you.

Hana-May Ghofoor (12)
All Saints CE Academy, Ingleby Barwick

No One Is Like You, No One Is Like Me

No one is like you, no one is like me
No one has your laugh, your smile, your looks
No one has your fingerprints, your thumbprint, your DNA
No one is like you, no one is like me
There is one of you and one of me
Even if you travel around the world you won't find anyone like you
There is only one of you and one of me
You're your own self because no one in this world is like you
Even twins, triplets, and families have differences
You are not the same as others
That's because everyone is different
You're your own self
No one is like you, no one is like me.

Harriett Hall (11)
All Saints CE Academy, Ingleby Barwick

Standards

Standards
What people believe in
Standards
What people try to fit into
But what if we didn't have to?
What if it was okay to look different?
What if it was okay to have flaws?
What if there were no expectations?
Standards
What if people's thoughts didn't put us through so much trouble?
What if we didn't spend hours scrolling through social media, comparing ourselves to other girls and boys
Who supposedly look 'better' than us
That look 'prettier' than us?
What if...
We are perfect just the way we are?

Alice McAvoy (11)
All Saints CE Academy, Ingleby Barwick

Be You

Be what you want to be
Everybody has a soul, make yourself useful
Own yourself
You might be great, nice, energetic, self-conscious,
Whatever you are, let the world know about you.
Be you.

About me. Likes and dislikes.
You are you
Everyone is different in their own way.
Just like each apple on a tree.
Some are round, some are big, small,
Whatever it is, it's okay.

Loads of people like things you don't,
What does it matter?
You are you and that's okay.

God's Favour Nwamba (11)

All Saints CE Academy, Ingleby Barwick

My Beautiful Truth

My beautiful truth is playing out with my friends,
Hoping that the fun will never end,
Looking back in time at the person you used to be,
Thinking, *wow look at me!*

My beautiful truth is my dream about gymnastics,
With flips and tricks all different sizes,
But we will have to see what the future brings!

My beautiful truth is my love for pizza and chicken nuggets,
Helping discrimination, equal rights and bullying,
Watching movies and television shows,
This is the real me!

Lois O'Keeffe (12)
All Saints CE Academy, Ingleby Barwick

21

Don't Fit In, Stand Out

Life is like a seed, we get planted
We grow like a fruit and eventually get eaten (die).
So that's why we have to
Enjoy life while it lasts
Now.
Life comes in differences, just like a fruit,
They are big, small and medium,
There are spotty fruits, and stripy fruits,
Now, you may be thinking,
Why am I talking about fruits,
It's because fruits symbolise our differences
If we are all the same we become boring,
So it's better to stand out than fit in, just like a fruit.

Zara Omakoji (12)

All Saints CE Academy, Ingleby Barwick

In Another World

In another world, everything would be okay
In another world, my auntie would be okay
In another world, you would've been given the blessing to be healthy
In another world, you would be able to finish 2024
In another world, maybe none of this would happen
In another world, I wouldn't have to watch you
Slowly pass away
In another world, illnesses wouldn't exist
In another world, I would've asked to see you more
In another world, maybe cancer wouldn't win.

Emelia Jeffries (12)
All Saints CE Academy, Ingleby Barwick

23

Needs To Change!

This needs to change,
Bullying is wrong.
More and more people get bullied every day,
People change because of the way they are,
As soon as people build their confidence up, people let them down.

The victims have their hopes and dreams high but then they change,
Tell a trusted adult about your problems,
So be different and ignore these rude people.
It's okay to be different,
So don't let them take you down.

Ellen Westerburg (11)
All Saints CE Academy, Ingleby Barwick

My Beautiful Truth

My beautiful truth, my beautiful truth, I wonder what it could be,
Could I be a footballer or a swimmer?
I will just have to wait and see.
This is my beautiful truth.
I could also be a doctor or a nurse.
I will just have to wait and see.
You know, I could be in a movie.
Harry Potter, The Mad Hatter or even The Lion King.
You will just have to wait and see.
This is my beautiful truth.

Tilly Dickens (11)
All Saints CE Academy, Ingleby Barwick

25

My Dream Your Dream

To my future self,
I believe we can achieve many goals.
Figure skating is the thing to focus on.
Just wait and see.
We shall shine bright.
I can feel it inside me.
We will both get there,
It is the truth.
When you look back in time,
You will see what I mean.
My dreams and your dreams are our life.
Our truth, our dreams, our hopes.
We will make it.
I know we will.

Holly Howsden (11)
All Saints CE Academy, Ingleby Barwick

Climbing Is A Commitment

People always have that one thing they're passionate about,
Whether it's a sport or a hobby,
For me, that was rock climbing.

I was committed,
That was my thing,
And the only thing that stopped me was the fear of falling.

If I could go back,
I'd tell myself that the fear of falling was only temporary,
And that the fear of not making it to the top was forever.

Adam Harkin (12)
All Saints CE Academy, Ingleby Barwick

Middlesbrough FC

You are my Boro
Win, lose or draw
I'm Boro to the core
As the turnstile doors open
We are ready to complete a battering
Teesiders ready, so am I
To sing our hearts out
'Cause I'm Boro till I die!

Jude Short (11)
All Saints CE Academy, Ingleby Barwick

My Beautiful Self

My beautiful truth
When you look back
What do you see?
This is me
Be yourself
Just be you
Be true

When times are hard
Power through
Be you
Be true.

Eliza Mayo (12)
All Saints CE Academy, Ingleby Barwick

The Beautiful Truth

What does friendship mean when we face strife?
What does fairness truly entail in life?
What is equality if it's yet to be found?
What is unity when we're divided all around?
What is happiness in a world filled with sorrow?
What is life if it's shrouded in darkness?
What could life be if it was intended to be all of those things?
It would be harmonic,
It would be cooperation,
It would be together,
And that's the beautiful truth.

Lucy Carkeek
Arnold Lodge School, Leamington Spa

The Unwritten Curriculum

School, a safe place,
Or so they say,
All these teachers on our case,
24/7, every day.

Where you can chase your dreams,
Or so they claim,
We're at the bottom of the hierarchy scheme.
Programming us to be the same,

They say we can express our emotions,
But in reality, they don't care,
They watch our every motion,
They say the rules are fair.

Children getting bullied on the daily,
Young and old,
Their minds ache and bleed,
They're like puppets being controlled.

They put tests on our table,
Increasing our stress,
They determine if we are able,
Putting our minds in a mess,

They call it school,
In reality, it's a teacher and student duel,
The face is the teachers,
We are the features.

Inaya Begum (14)
Arts & Media School, Islington

31

Growing Up

I used to be small, just a kid at play
Chasing my friends, laughing all day
The world felt so big, full of magic and light
Every adventure was a pure delight

Now I'm getting taller, and things are changing fast
With homework and choices, it's a whole new cast
Sometimes I feel lost, trying to find my way
Learning to be me in this brand-new sway

I still love to dream and play in the sun
But growing up's weird, and it's just begun
Through all of the ups and the crazy downs
I'm finding my voice and wearing my crown

Embracing the journey, come what may,
I'll take every challenge, day by day.

Yusuf Mohamed Ben Ali (13)
Arts & Media School, Islington

On Repeat

I wake up in the morning,
With a smile on my face,
Nothing's really boring,
I've just gotta keep up the pace.

I get out of bed,
And put my shoes on,
When I stand up, I get dizzy,
Don't know what's going on.

I leave for school,
And go to meet up with my friends.
I've known these guys forever,
We're together 'til the end.

At the end of the day,
I go back to sleep,
And wake up in the morning,
Just for this life to repeat.

Eleanor Murray (13)
Arts & Media School, Islington

From Sand To Stone

From Qatar's golden sand, they flew
A family of eight, dreams bright and new
Where the sun shone warm and life was sweet
Now England's streets beneath their feet.

The father works, though times are tough
In a land where nothing comes easy enough
But still, they laugh, they still hold tight
And make new memories in the London night.

A three-day trip, the citywide
They marvelled at the London pride
Big Ben, stood stall, the tower gleamed
And for a while, life felt like a dream.

Though struggles grow like winter's chill
They share their love, they share their will
In every storm, they find the calm
In every trial, a steady palm.

The cost of living may bite and sting
But in their hearts, they feel the spring
They remember skies of desert gold
And carry warmth when nights are cold.

The father knows he's not alone
For family's love is always home
Though Qatar's sands are far away
In England's rain, they find their way.

Together, together, they push ahead
With hope and joy in every tear shed
For even in this foreign place
They find the strength, they find the grace.

Rumaisah Ahmed (13)
Barton Court Grammar School, Canterbury

Cars Are Freedom

Cars are freedom.
They can get you anywhere you want, ten times faster than walking.
They can be electric, or the dirtiest diesel.
They can be white, or the blackest of blacks.
Cars can be huge, or they can be tiny.
Cars can cost millions or just a few hundred pounds.
Two-wheeled, three-wheeled, four-wheeled, six-wheeled.
The variety is never-ending.
I watch them drive past my bedroom window.
Dreaming of owning an Aston Martin, a Ferrari, a Lamborghini.
They take me to a world of my own.
Lying in bed seeing the first corner.
On the race track going two hundred miles an hour.
On the country roads at sixty.
Even driving down the local streets at thirty.
Cars aren't just my hobby, they're my life.
The design of the wheels, the headlights, the engines.
A purring V6, a growling V12, a roaring V8 or a thundering V10.
Speeding down the cold, hard tar,
Driving in my car that can get me far.

Jasper Drysdale (12)

Bishop Vesey's Grammar School, Sutton Coldfield

Racism Is Bad

Let me set the record straight,
We're off to rise above, eradicate the hate,
Different colours, different faces,
But under the skin, we're all the human race,
Unity in diversity, that's the key,
Respect for all, let's live in harmony,
Let's break down the walls, and tear down the fences,
Together we stand against all offences,
It's time to speak up, make a change,
Won't stay silent in the face of rage,
We're stronger than that, that's a fact,
No room for hate, got to counteract,
Unity in diversity, that's the key,
Respect for all, let's live in harmony,
Let's break down the walls and tear down the fences,
Together we stand against all offences.

Rithvik Deepak (13)
Bishop Vesey's Grammar School, Sutton Coldfield

37

The Mirage Of Tomorrow

A future bleak, under shadows cast
Where echoes of hope dissolve too fast
Screens blink, a web of fractured light
The heart grows cold in endless night
Eyes strain, seeking meaning lost
In this digital sea, souls exhaust
The tether tightens, and the spirit prays
Bound to illusion, we count the days
No voice, no dreams to mend
In this hollow world, we descend
Connection falters, trust betrayed
A sterile life in wires arrayed
Scroll on and on, without an end
Humanity forgotten, no will to defend
The future withers, truth unwound
In virtual chains, forever bound.

Ryan Thomas (12)
Bishop Vesey's Grammar School, Sutton Coldfield

Farming Life

Up when the sun rises
And out on the fields
Lie all the animals
Waiting to start their day
One foggy morning
Going across the field on my quad bike
I stop in the silence to check they're all okay
I shake my cake bag
The sheep all come running to me
Diamond, Pearl and Betsy are all pleased to see me
I give them their food and set off on my way
To go back to the farm
To collect the tractor and the bales of hay
I set off again to go back to the field
To put the hay in the ring feeder
Lucy, Mellisa, IT Girl and I'm A Beaut
Come running over to see what's to eat
Now that they're fed and watered and full
It's time for me to get started with my day
Home for a shower, breakfast and dressed
Off to school where there will be no rest
After school, it's the sheep again, time for more cake
Then feeding the dogs and watch a bit of TV
Now I'm off to bed before it all begins again
There's no rest when you're a farmer.

Tommy Holmes (11)
Cartmel Priory CE School, Cartmel

39

A Great Invention

This great creation that I speak of,
Could only really be one thing,
The invention of the train, no one really thinks of,
Yet this invention was a saviour,
The creation of the steam train allows more travel,
Originating from Manchester, going to Liverpool,
The first two cities linked by rail.

Over time, this idea grew and grew,
Until steam was left alone,
Trains now running all over the world,
Most powered by electricity, some by magnetism,
The fastest train belongs to Japan,
Trains will keep developing,
Keep getting faster,
However, things are lost in this change.

These things that are lost,
Such as coals and controls,
They're all replaced but some things still seem to be lost,
Trains used to run with tonnes of fun metal pipes,
Now all that's left is a button in their place.

Trains used to be so much fun to control,
Now just another boring chore,
This wonderful creation in my opinion,
Has been ruined over the years,
If only steam had another chance.

Joe Elson (13)
Cartmel Priory CE School, Cartmel

Hooks

Lonely but not alone,
Loved but never cherished,
They sit and watch her sparkle perish,
Sat in a group,
Laughing and smiling,
Can't they see her slowly dying?
Sly whispers and looks,
Driving like hooks,
Into her brain,
Causing her pain,
Dissecting situations,
Overthinking conversations,
But going without her won't matter, will it?
Every time they do, it dampens her spirit,
Her wish to be valued,
Even for a day,
She's certain it will drive the hooks far away,
But it's a pathetic attempt,
Their love was spent,
Sometimes the hooks seem to loosen their grip,
But then one hurtful nip,
A small tether,
And suddenly they're back,
And deeper than ever.

Lola Newton (13)
Cartmel Priory CE School, Cartmel

We Are All Human

It doesn't matter if you're fat or thin, small or tall,
You have loads of hair or you are bald,
You are young or old, dark or light.
It doesn't matter what you look like or who you are.
We are all human.

So maybe if you see someone who looks different
Just say hello or even smile
Remember they're a person too.
Just because someone doesn't look like you
It doesn't mean they are any different.

Remember we are all the same.
Who knows, maybe talking to them might actually be fun
So if you do see someone different
Just be nice and smile and remember
We are all human.

Toby Kendall (11)
Cartmel Priory CE School, Cartmel

Dance

Dance is me,
I am dance,
It sets me free,
While I prance.

My emotions are heavy,
Heavy as a rock,
Dance is the key,
The key to my lock.

My life is worthless,
Worthless without dance,
My life would be a mess,
But with it, I have a chance.

Without dance,
Where would I be?
Sad and angry,
Most probably.

Dance is me,
I am dance,
It sets me free,
While I prance.

Abi Kendall (12)
Cartmel Priory CE School, Cartmel

44

Heinz Beans

Beans oh beans, I do love Heinz beans
You can have them on toast, you can have them with cheese
Sometimes I think my blood's made of beans
Never will I stop eating beans
If I stopped then life wouldn't be
If you like beans, then we can be friends
We can eat beans together until the day ends
To the inventor of Heinz I just want to say
When I eat your beans, it just makes my day!

Lennon Daggett (12)
Cartmel Priory CE School, Cartmel

Fluctuate

In the silence of dusk,
A white flower weeps,
Petals pale like forgotten dreams,
Each droplet of rain a tear,
Beauty haunted by loss,
Fragile bloom,
A whisper of sorrow,
Hope turned to shadow,
Sunlight set to darkness,
The sound of talking to the sound of silence,
Bravery reduced to fear,
Happiness swapped with dread,
And the saying, "Help me."
Swapped with the lie, "I'm okay."
And yet after all,
I still feel the slight spark,
I feel so confused,
As to why my emotions always fluctuate.

Harvey Lewis (15)
Corby Technical School, Corby

Frozen In Time

As I was watching the bell,
Waiting for it to ring,
My heart was beating fast,
I couldn't listen to a thing,
The time was going slowly,
But somehow it came closely,
Until now!
Did the clock stop?
Why was everyone frozen?
Oh, I forgot,
Could I move?
Oh, yes I could.

As I removed my blazer,
I noticed something,
What is it? I wondered,
What is it?
It was pink,
Glowing,
Like a star in the sky,
Wait, is it day or night? I couldn't remember,
As I walked towards it, I shuddered,
Thud!
I hit the floor,
My eyes flickered as they opened,
What happened?
Wait, I was back in my seat,

Everything was moving again?
What happened?
Thud!
Wait, that wasn't me...

Erin (11)
Court Fields School, Wellington

This Is Human Life

In a world of billions of people, I live
Well or healthy of which nobody shows concern of
I die from my own spirit and awareness
Conscious of who I am, how I look, what I say or see or know
or knew

It's my past
I am told to embrace it but I am condemned for it
Being taught to adopt hatred and regret all summed up in a
negative language
Because this is what is commonly known as 'life'
And pain just another word for a day
Of what humane feelings gush out of my heart
As sympathy for those before and after me though I am told
to say nothing

Judge or be judged is the only motto to live by
As a friend can become a foe to a stranger all in the name
of self-protection and a guarded heart
To what do we owe ourselves this bondage life cycle
Where all our knowledge, clouded by our own false
jurisdiction even of ourselves, we have no rule

Let me be first to question morality on the ground of faux
comparison only as a sign of criticism all in the name of
wisdom
That one is wiser than the rest because of a past life case
study

That those to come are not only fledglings to the industry
But baggage to the old

Modern rule now insulted by a past who knows no bound
And to speak of self-care and health on the grounds of
exfoliators and
Polishes that tone the skin but leave the mind
To look admirable on the outside but ugly on the inner
Of a world where only two kinds exist
The dumb and the stupid of which we fall under the latter

For my future
I am told to look up to the sky for a bright light even when
The rain pours ahead
The type that clatters above me as a feeling rather than a
sound
I hold my breath
Imagination to run wild because I feel as though I can do all
In a split second my hopes are up
Encouraging music to fuel my unstable mind that all is well

That I will live to see a happy ending
I think
That I will no longer struggle in life for as long as I...
Make everything a joke
'Don't take yourself too seriously'
But who will if I choose not to?

As my present
I will suffer
The weight of the world on my shoulders
Listen to what others say or tell me
That I may one day do the same
To question nothing but my identity
Because...

Who am I?
I am the girl who cried yesterday
I am the boy who lies every day
But no
For I am none
For I am what is commonly known but uncommonly
understood
Famous excuse for mistakes
I am *human.*

Oluwadamilola Adekeye (17)
Culford School, Culford

The Land Of The Giants

I come from the land of the giants,
Where every head rises above the clouds,
And, all of these heads were sincerely reliant
On the little white bees that fly in the trees,
That I have grown up to love.

They keep sickness at bay,
And keep us merry all day.
As they buzz their sweet bee song,
Singing all night and day long.

Though they require just one thing,
A tooth from the giant's almighty grin.

But if the giants don't give it that day,
The bees will go and fetch it themselves.
They'll take their axes and with a battle cry, they say,
"These giants aren't giants, they're acting like elves,
Fetch me what is rightfully ours!"

Rosie Carter (14)
Frome College, Frome

The Truth

This is the truth.
The world is changing rapidly.
The past five years have been different from the rest.
KSI's new song, 'The Thick of It', has been getting hate.
Skibidi toilet has brainwashed the minds of young people.
This makes it worse for the next generation.
The more time goes on, the worse it gets.
Technology is moving fast.
The world is changing rapidly.
This is the truth.

Louie Nicholls (13)
Frome College, Frome

Dream Big Or Go Home

I dream, you dream, everyone dreams,
I dream maybe one day I'll soar up in the sky,
Feeling free, feeling fresh, feeling full of might,
I'll look down to Earth and shout, "Yoo-hoo!"
Oh, I hope I'll be able to achieve it, I do!
I will gaze upon the starry sky,
Up in my rocket,
Flying ever so high,
The sun will smile at me with a warm loving gleam,
Congratulating me on accomplishing my dream,

Or I dream I could be an awesome scientist, scanning the
charts,
Talking about biology and anatomy parts,
I would dissect animals and examine bodies,
I would analyse data and continuously study,
I would be a radical genius,
Cooped up in my lab,
With my long lovely lab coat and testing tubes,
I would be lenient with my colleagues and work with them
well,
I'd feel like a magician crafting spells,

Or I dream maybe I could be an incredible policewoman,
Gun in hand,
Defending justice with my badge gleaming in the sun,
Protecting the innocent and punishing the bad,

54

Seeing what's wrong,
I'd protect the people with my slick ninja moves,
Hiya!
Pow!
Bam!
With my team I'd search for clues,
Looking for footprints and fingerprints too,

Or I dream maybe I could be a talented actress,
I'd throw the audience into laughter and act with my heart
and soul,
Acting any given role,
I would be a grumpy old granny,
With my handbag as my weapon,
Or I'd be a villain,
With my magic staff in hand,
Or a cool dude just chillin',
Whatever I was I would give it my all,
I love to express myself,
In any way possible,
Thinking about that...

I dream I could be an artist,
I'd paint abstract art,
Creating the war using black, white and red,
The blood, the gore, the lying dead,
Or I could paint my thoughts and feelings like,
Multicoloured polka dots,

Or bright neon squiggly lines,
Adding a new colour every time,
Maybe I would use the cross-hatching technique,
I'd draw anime faces or animals too,
Whatever comes to mind I'll do,

In fact, now I think about it,
What about a rugby player?
Oh, how I love rugby,
I love my team, my friends, the sport,
We work together and give each other the best support,
One united, pushing to score the try,
The intensity,
"Tackle, ruck! Who's there, who's there?"
Then, "Spread out, spread out!"
We laugh together when we've made mistakes or scored a
brilliant try,
And we support and feel each other's pain when they are
hurt, upset or crying,
But we also encourage each other through ups and downs,
We're in it together,
Through it all,
Thick and thin,
Short and tall,

It doesn't matter one bit at all,
Whether your dream is big or small,
So go!

Dream big or go home,
Dream big,
Dream hard,
Don't give up no matter what life throws at us,
Don't make a fuss,
You'll strive through and stay strong,
Knowing your dream all along,
It stays in your head and sits tight and firm,
For you to keep in mind,
And in your moments of self-doubt you can remember,
That that dream is there forever,

So go!
Dream big or go home!
Dream big,
And dream hard,
Don't give up,

Good luck!

Micaela Constantino (12)
Heathside School, Weybridge

The Truth

In a world full of lies and cries, of faking smiles
Wearing a special style is the life

Where fakery is everywhere and authenticity is a gem so rare,
So cherish those who care
Because in this world there are lots of snares
So love your loved ones and don't be scared

In this world of pretence and show
Your real friends will shine and even glow
Don't believe some things you see
Being real is a priceless seal
Be unique and not in a crowd
Don't believe and you will be proud

So be yourself and not someone else
You will succeed and nothing less
Believe in yourself and not your mirror
Trust me, it's a real thriller.

Kathryn King (12)
Highfields School, Penn

School

Education, one step at a time
Take a big leap, it will slow down your time
School, hell hole and prison
All big words
Just for some education.

Cain Brady (12)
ISCA Academy, Exeter

Cold-Blooded Murderers

The blood fills the streets
As people fall like flies

As the cruel, conniving murderer
Scours for its next victim
Searching around
But the question is, why?

Why do they kill?
Why now?
Why this victim?
What will happen now?

The victim is secured
All they have to do is kill!

The victim not knowing
What nightmare is about to come...

As the room fills with screams
Silence hits the room

They are more sinister than the devil
Yet they will be given a short sentence
And will be allowed to breathe the fresh air.

Raheece Alikhan (13)
Joseph Leckie Academy, Walsall

Melton Foxes

Maybe we were just the better team,
Maybe winning is our new theme,
We used to lose every game,
Now our names are going up with fame,
we scored eight, they scored zero,
Loads of our players are heroes,
One thing that I know is that we won,
And another is that it was fun.

At the beginning, bad,
But at the end, they were mad,
I nearly scored their goals,
And got loads of wows,
I guess soon,
My dreams won't be dreams.

Marcel Klause (12)
Long Field Spencer Academy, Melton Mowbray

Miss You, Grandad

In the sky,
So wide and blue,
I look for you, Great Grandad,
It's true.

When the raindrops fall,
And the sun peeks out,
I see your smile,
There's never a doubt.

The rainbows stretch,
Across the sky,
Colours dancing,
Oh so high!

In the pitter-patter of the rain,
I hear your laughter,
Sweet as a train,
You told me stories,
Old and wise,
Now, I find you in the bright, blue skies.

Though you're not here,
I feel you near,
In every rainbow,
I hold you dear,
With every colour,

I feel it's true,
I remember you.

So, when it rains,
And the world feels grey,
I'll look for your colours,
That light my way.

In my heart,
You'll always stay,
My happy memories,
Come out to play.

Layla Addesso-Arthur (12)
Long Field Spencer Academy, Melton Mowbray

Football

Maybe we were tired,
Maybe we had too many days off,
I know that we could have played harder.

Maybe we were not ready.
Maybe.

On Sunday I played a match,
It was Assordby vs Foxes.
We started praying on my couch,
Said to us, come on girls,
We can win today!
I felt strong but they scored,
By the end it was 5-1,
We lost.
Maybe we were tired,
Maybe we had too many days off,
I know that we could have done better.

I don't think we were ready.
It was half time,
We still had more time to quickly pass the ball,
Then we started playing.
A new goalie went in our goal,
So we shot two goals in ten minutes

Until it was 5-4,
We still had time
For the other team to win.

Isabella O'Flaherty
Long Field Spencer Academy, Melton Mowbray

The Forests

As the falling leaves came out of the trees
The waving grass fell straight asleep.
All the squirrels sat up the trees
As the hushing water calmed the bees.
The crunch of the autumn leaves
Soothed the tiny critters beneath
As wolves gnashed at others with their teeth.
The sun goes down and so do the worms
Returning to what they call Earth.
This poem is finished and so am I, now
It's time to say goodbye.

Kanisha Valentine (12)
Looe Community Academy, East Looe

Trauma

How fast can your life change?
The answer is as fast as the wind. Why?
That's just the way life is...

It goes from minor to major. It's a spiral.
Why can't the spiral be stopped?
It's an addiction and there's no prediction.
But it's fine, right? It's only you that it affects, right?

The answer to that is: it's not true. Why?
It affects family and friends too. Why?

Imagine a 200-piece puzzle,
One piece doesn't matter, right?
There are 199 other pieces,
But that's wrong. Why?

You can't have a complete puzzle
Without that one piece.

Connor Pile (15)
North Herts ESC, Letchworth

67

Dazzling Rainbow

A rainbow is like an arch.
A rainbow is very nice and colourful.
A rainbow makes us feel nice and dazzly.
A rainbow is as big as an animal.

Zubaydah Hassan

Oakwood Specialist College, Yate

The Power Of Love Helps

Every time I see her all I can see is struggle
and all I want to do is snuggle.
Time and time again, all I can see is pain,
So before I walk away I ask about her day.

Every time she gets ignored it makes my heart ache
So every night I'm awake, picturing her tear-filled face
and that makes the tears grow on the inside, and flow on
the outside.

Now I understand so that the tears can slow down
but still, I can see her pain, which makes a faint tear fall.
Eventually, the pain will fade
but for now, it's the same.

Every time I see her all I can see is struggle
and all I want to do is snuggle.
Time and time again, all I see is pain,
So before I walk away I ask about her day.

Nathan Ford (12)
Poole High School, Poole

Fake Identity

What do you see? Do you see what I see?
The world behind the camera
Do you believe what you see?
Do your senses have a mind of their own?
The world behind the camera is what I call home
Do your inspirations and idols act how they claim to?
Or do you just believe the world that only you can see?

Is your world real or is it fake?
How do you know what you see isn't just a mistake?
Do you know whether your idols make you feel jealous,
unhappy or sad?
Don't you want their life to be yours to make you happy and
glad?

No matter how much I try, I can't change how you want to
be
But I can change me and not have a fake identity.

Amelie Silveira (12)
Poole High School, Poole

Don't Give Up On Your Dreams

You should never give up on your dreams
Because if you really enjoy doing that thing you do
And something happens to you like getting badly hurt
When you have recovered you should try it again.
This has happened to me when I was scooting
I fell and split my lip
And I was going to quit scooting
Till I did a trick
I fell on and I did not fall that time
And now I am ten times better at scooting
This quote can change lives.

George Christou (12)
Poole High School, Poole

In Reality

T he truth is good
R are things make it bad
U ndermine the bad things
T hen the truth will appear
H ere is the truth which isn't bad.

Caspar Dade (13)
Poole High School, Poole

My Dog

T erribly cute
E veryone's friend
D on't you dare leave me
D on't you dare cry
Y ou know you're loved and you know why.

Elisha Reid (13)
Poole High School, Poole

Truth

The day I murdered them
I got away with it at least for now.
On the outside, I seem like the average Joe,
But inside a dark, dark secret possesses my body,
eats at me.
I don't regret it.
It fuels me. It helps. I want to kill again.
Some would think it's a gut-wrenching feeling.
Not for me: I enjoyed the lifeless body in front of me
Exciting
So very exciting.

Aiden Platt (15)

Regents Park Community College, Regents Park

Love Story

We were both young when I first saw you
And Mummy said, "Go say hi to her,"
And I started crying saying, "I don't want to go."
Then I said, "Hi, my name is Juliet, what is yours?"
And then we started talking.

We became good friends
And we never let each other go away,
And then we started dating.

And then, Father told me that love is a feeling
When someone gives you everything
And will be willing to stay with you
Through every hard thing.

Then, prom came
And I thought at first that you were going to choose me
But we broke up and I felt something in my heart.
It felt like I should never trust anyone.

But my mum told me that I should never give up
And I believed her.
I started dating someone else and she saved me.
I felt happy again, like there was still hope in life.
Thank you.

Tamaraseri Andrea Brisihe (11)
Seaham High School, Seaham

Alone Never

Sometimes I wonder
If I'm truly alone
Throughout Earth and space
But then I realise
I'm never alone
The flowers have petals
The animals have mates
The solar system has stars
And I remember
I'm never alone.

H Belton (13)
Sir John Hunt Community Sports College, Whitleigh

The Struggles Of Cats

"Get a cat," they said,
"It will be a laugh!" they said,
They were wrong!

When I got my cat, he thwacked my rat as hard as a bat,
Rest in peace, Matt the rat!
I bought my cat a £60 bed,
It was very comfortable and was bright red,
What did he do?
He slept in the box that the bed came in!
"Boohoo!" I said.

Don't think that's the end,
Don't put your cat on your head!
Your cat may be a good hat,
But if you don't give him good pats,
He will probably scratch your face and bite your hair,
Till there is no more left!

Don't be put off getting a cat, as they may be a struggle.
They will always give you good snuggles and cuddles.

Spencer Kerr (13)
Solway Community Technology College, Silloth

Who Are We?

Who are we?... Who are you?
We can be anyone, and you can be anyone.
Different people see you differently.
To some, you might be 'a bully',
but to others, you could be the sweetest person ever.
Maybe to yourself, you're neither.
But the point is you can be anyone.
Anyone you think you are.
You can be a different person every day.
People change all the time.
People change their appearance, attitude, lovers,
interests, and so much more.
So, who are you? Who are you to yourself?

Mimi Morgan (11)
Solway Community Technology College, Silloth

My Dog

My dog is really funny,
Her fur is really curly.
She wants to bounce like a bunny,
And go round in twirly whirlys.

My dog is very silly,
She can act really crazy.
One day she bit into a chilli,
Then she turned a bit shady.

My dog is very cuddly,
Her fur is soft and warm.
Everyone says she's lovely,
And she protects me from a storm.

Tammy Morris Crawford (13)
Solway Community Technology College, Silloth

The Truth

M y favourite thing to do is spend time with my friends
Y ou do what you do and I'll do what I do

L ove, I love my family, my mam, dad, brother and sister
I support Man City because it's my favourite club
F ootball is my favourite sport because it is fun
E njoy, I enjoy playing football and watching boxing.

Bradley Baxter (11)
Solway Community Technology College, Silloth

True Beauty

T reatment,
R espect others and what they look like, be
U nique as you can,
E ncourage each other.

B eauty is everything,
E lectrolysis,
A mazing looks,
U be who you want to be, be
T rue to yourself,
Y ou are beautiful with or without make-up.

Bridget Irwin (13)

Solway Community Technology College, Silloth

True Friends

The truth is if you have false friends,
Don't let them walk all over you.

If they do, then don't let them walk all over you,
And if they do, just walk away.
One day, just say,
"I don't want to be friends anymore."

Leah Emmerson (11)
Solway Community Technology College, Silloth

Sunsets

S tunning like a shooting star
U nique, just like me
N ice like my dog
S parkly like glitter
E legant like a swan on a pond
T he beauty of sunsets.

Maisie Emmerson (13)

Solway Community Technology College, Silloth

I Believe That People Should Believe In Their Own Opinions

I believe people shouldn't feel down
And shouldn't drown.
I believe people should believe in their opinions
And shouldn't believe in anyone else's.
I believe.

Maisie Stalker (11)
Solway Community Technology College, Silloth

Our Loving Companions

In fields where flowers bloom and trees sway,
Dogs frolic and bark, eager to play.
Eyes shining bright,
Playful from morning 'til light.

With fur so soft and hearts so kind,
A sense of peace you'll definitely find.
They chase the wind, they fetch the ball,
With not a care in the world at all.

Through fields they run, through rivers they swim,
In every adventure, they gleefully join in.
Their playfulness brings laughter and cheer,
In moments of sadness they always draw near.

With noses that sniff each scent in the air,
They explore, they explore the world without a care.
So here's to dogs, our loyal friends,
A bond unbroken, a love that never ends.

Charlie Edge (14)
Spalding Grammar School, Spalding

Making A Perfect Tea

Step one,
Pour water in with fun,
Let it boil,
Make sure the bubbles are ready to pop, like coils.

Step two,
Get the book,
Winnie the Pooh,
Ready to read,
Ready to pull the weeds.

Step three,
Grab the PG Tips for the tea,
Soak one in the water for a few minutes,
Never forget to count the digits.

Step four,
Now pour some milk, and never ignore,
Allow it to bubble and pop,
Hop on the laptop.

Step five,
Ready for work and to arrive,
A light pinch of sugar for some relish,
Now enjoy and dwell in.

Ayaan Asim-Ellahi (11)
Spalding Grammar School, Spalding

The Truth, By Maximilian

I'm the only person that cares about the homeless,
By giving a pound or more.
I believe in the process of life, that there will be lots of
problems.
But I never give up on my dreams.
I don't care what team I support.
I support that team I'm proud of (Man City).
The last bit about my truth is that,
People that come from a different country are still loving
and caring.
But this world is not having that opportunity.
I hope this world will change in the next years.

Maximilian Kolodziejczyk (13)
Spalding Grammar School, Spalding

Music

Music
All music is
Different, nothing is
Really the same. Just sit
Down and listen, and I will change
The way. You think this poem is about
Music. Well, that could be true. Emotions are like music,
You can go from pop to blues. Hip-hop, rap and drill could
be making
You feel red, but why be so worked up when you can be
mellow
Instead. Rhythm is important, it
Keeps your life in balance, fall out
Of it and you may lose
Your talents. Be the
Music to people's
Ears. Follow your dreams
And passions, don't copy
Your peers.

Kirsty Pone (14)
St Ambrose Barlow RC High School, Wardley

Did She Love Me Enough?

The rain on the car is like therapy
My heavy breathing
Pant and pant
As I drive through a field full of her favourite flowers
My eyes swell with pain as
Tears pile up
Sometimes I think she is there
Patting me on the back
Saying how proud she is of me.

She showed me how everyone inside is unique
She taught me the ways of being a lady
And being kind
She made me laugh but was that enough?
I held her hand
I felt the loving soul leave her
I fell to my knees
It's okay, I will halt
You can go now, Nan
I will grow up and be unique
I played back the memories
It hit me hard
But my question was
Did I love her enough
I'm older now
I grew and I knew it was because of you.

Freya Duggan (12)
St Andrew's CE High School, Worthing

89

Home

Home is where I belong
Home is where I find my song
Home is where I fit in
Home is where I am with my mum, my dad and my sister
Home is where I can do my hobbies
Home is where I belong
Apples and pears are sweet
No eyes no ears
This is not my home
Home is where I find my song
Ants are strong
They have eyes but more than two legs
I do not belong
Home is where I relax
Dogs are smart but they have four legs
I don't belong
Home is where I'm with my family
My parents have two legs and two eyes
I have their genes
I do belong and I am home.

Frankie Morris (12)
St Andrew's CE High School, Worthing

Netball Is My Therapy

Swish, swash, schwoop the sound of the netball going
through the hoop.
Netball is my therapy, I live and love netball.
I take a turn for the ball. I take a turn for my team.
I make a difference in what people see of me, netball is my
therapy.
Everyone says teamwork is the dreamwork,
Ever since I have played with my team we have got closer
and closer together.
Since I have played netball we have gotten closer and closer
to that prize.
Whenever I think of us as a team it fills my eyes with tears.

Netball is a journey you must be willing to take.

Netball is my therapy!

Niamh Francis (12)
St Andrew's CE High School, Worthing

Untitled

The day is dead,
The night is dark,
I'm lying here,
Stuck in my own head,
My thoughts echo,
My stomach twists.

I want to sleep,
I want the thoughts to go,
But they're always there,
Does anyone even care?

The tears begin to fall,
My breath becomes heavy,
The thoughts grow louder,
Will it ever stop?

Am I just weak?
Is this normal?
Am I twisted?
Am I dramatic?

Can it all stop?
Can I put it to bed?
The more I cry,
The more my eyes go red.

Poppy Logsdon (13)
St Andrew's CE High School, Worthing

Darkness And Suffocated Souls

Darkness
To light
Frozen flowers crack under my feet
Flowers aren't alone
A world full of people, yet I feel alone
Suffocated.

Darkness to light
It's dinnertime
No one talks
They just eat
I'll break a glass to have something other than silence
Suffocated.

Darkness
The stars shine bright
No one's awake
But I hear the rain outside
Suffocated
Darkness stays dark.

Sophie Ayrey (13)
St Andrew's CE High School, Worthing

Listening

Like therapy to my ears
Like a world without sound
Volume on loud, wait there's sound?
I plug my earphones in
The stress drains out
Rhythm and harmony come in and out
I'm proud
Proud of the peace
Proud of the love
Proud of the passion and being above
Above all the hate
Above all the meanness
Above all the meaningless things, just being free.

Carys Booth (13)
St Andrew's CE High School, Worthing

Untitled

Foxes are mysterious
Foxes are fascinating
Foxes are like a familiar friend
Foxes are like a door to the forest
Foxes are wild
When I see a fox, I think of a calm, cold, dark morning
Just before the sun rises.

Alex Hatton (12)
St Andrew's CE High School, Worthing

Lip Gloss

Sticky, shiny, slick.
The taste of fresh strawberries.
Reminds me of a summer picnic.
Has a texture like slime.
Makes my smile glow.
Gloss, glitter and glow
Makes them glimmer.

Poppy McConnell (13)
St Andrew's CE High School, Worthing

The Beautiful Truth

I once thought life was beautiful,
Oh, if only I'd have known.
An infant bird falls from its nest,
Right there upon the road,
Wrong place, wrong time.
Machines start to queue, impatience,
If only the foremost vehicle was mine.
Now agitated eyes meet,
Should I leave my vehicle? Help?
Pick up the little one? Too late.
The devil drives him forward,
Life is beautiful? Pure lies.

Ellie Quinn (17)
St Bees School, St Bees

Be Kind

B eing kind is the best you can be,
E ven though you're having a bad day, still be kind,

K indness is great, happiness is better,
I nspirational people will go far,
N ice people feel good to be around,
D edicated to being kind is a good thing,

T rustworthy people are great,
O utstanding is a good thing to be,

O ptimistic is not bad either,
T alented people feel good to be around,
H eroic people save lives,
E xtraordinary people do well in their grades,
R elaxed people are calm,
S uperior people make the world go round!

Oscar Robinson (11)
St Ives School, Higher Tregenna

Life's Truth

When the heart stops throbbing.
When the body becomes frail.
When the skin starts sobbing,
And blows in the saddening gale.
Then man has to face,
Face-to-face, life's horrible face.
No soul, no feeling, no breath,
The ultimate truth of life is death.
When one dies, he becomes history.
His soul departs, leaving behind a futile carcass.
An empty mind as death remains a mystery.
The ones that are left behind, are left with pain.
The ones that are gone, are laid to rest.
The ones on the ground, pray for their death.
How they are, that's unknown.
It's up to their faith and heart to decide.

Kade Mountain (12)
St Ives School, Higher Tregenna

Do You Understand?

I was thinking about what really bothers me.
As a human, we never really see.
You and I have equal rights.
But humanity seems to turn a blind eye.
Because when it comes to our mind,
Others just turn to the wrong side.
And when my hands become paws,
And when my shades become colours,
Is when the crowd turns red,
And glares at one another.
This needs to stop. Why can't we accept each other?
In silence we suffer.
But for the last time, I'll ask you,
"Do you understand the truth of this fight?"
The truth of this light.
The truth is *our* life...

Alana Harding (11)
St Ives School, Higher Tregenna

Colours In Our Rainbow

Red is like a shiny gorgeous ruby you find in a shimmering treasure chest.
Orange is like a juicy, tasty orange that you find in a fruit tree.
Yellow is as gorgeous as a piece of gold jewellery.
Green is as stunning as an emerald you can find in a stone shop.
Blue is as vibrant as a summer sky.
Purple is like a sweet, juicy plum.
Pink is like a stick of tasty cotton candy you find in a carnival.

Jessica Shellard (11)
St John Baptist CIW High School, Aberdare

Society

I woke up today and brushed my teeth;
I took a shower and ate brekkie.
I prepared my bag and did my homework and put on my uniform,
ready for school's work.
I said bye to my mother and stepped out the front door.
I was secretly dreading and dreading evermore.
And as I put my AirPods in,
my surroundings changed as they always did,
the fear and dread replaced by dear mania,
happily, as my mind said and said that the happiness gets rid of my anxiety and it's so fulfilling,
though the music is temporary.
As I step into school and take the AirPods out,
Besides me, it feels as if my mind is swelling,
so many people,
so much judgement,
so, in this wretched place, can I really be me?
As the day flies by, the anxiety of a separate being simply just looking and judging me,
I feel as if the dread just gets worse and worse
and though it does,
though it feels like a curse,
I know that I'll soon be home free
but I'm reminded that there are so many others just like me,
perhaps maybe another boy in my class

or maybe the teacher teaching the class?
So many questions held inside me,
held inside me.

But society,
it expects me to repeat itself utterly, sadly -
to work a 9-5 job just to live.
Woe to me,
as a primary, secondary, tertiary fuelling society.

I dread,
they dread,
I see,
they see,
but are things really the way they seem to be?
Does perhaps even the leader of a nation fear like me?
As day after day and the work repeats -
society expects us to simply be happy?
Suffering continues as a red sea forms
as people die sadly and smoke forms;
we are uncertain about things for certain,
soon society may not exist anymore.

Liam Carter (12)
St John Baptist CIW High School, Aberdare

I Believe

I believe that the world can be a better place
if we all try to make it one
that there can be no war, no crime and hatred
I believe that if we all do our best
we will no longer have to worry about our future
because we will not have to overthink anything
or be scared about what the world will become
I believe we can change the world
one step at a time.

Chloe Williams (13)
St John Baptist CIW High School, Aberdare

School

S ometimes we don't like school, but it can be good,

C ome and make your life a better place to live in,

H elp each other learn and life will be much easier,

O pen up the gates to your future,

O pen up the gate to school,

L ook at everyone and tell them school is nice.

Teddy Cresswell (12)
St John Baptist CIW High School, Aberdare

Why?

Why don't the stars glimmer anymore?
We could have looked upon the shine of shooting stars,
Now there's just a black dark sky.

Elsie Patterson (13)
St John Baptist CIW High School, Aberdare

Hopes And Passion

B race yourselves like you brace others.

E very time, interact with others like you already know the person.

L ove yourselves like you love people.

I ntelligence is all we need as students.

E ncouragement is key to all of us.

V oice in all of us, speak out loud.

E volving the things in me.

I ntegrity - always doing the right thing

N ow is the time we go for gold.

Y our life is yours, don't let anyone define it.

O utstanding effort in everything.

U nderstanding everything around you.

R elevant - set goals.

S urprise yourself, express yourself.

E ffort in everything.

L ower your temper.

F or those you care for, my family.

Mojola Olayode (12)

St Patrick's Catholic College, Thornaby

My Beautiful House

My house is great, my house is great, it lies in Thornaby,
My house, my house, in my house, there's everything you need.
My house is great, that's no debate.

Nowhere is better, my house is the best,
My bed, my Xbox, my phone and snacks,
Also a dog,
What else is going on?
There's my kitchen and living room,
Oh, there's so much more.
I've stayed there for thirteen years,
My house, oh my house,
My bedding is great,
Just like my clothes, they stayed.

In my room lies Dr Pepper, crisps, chocolate, plus my bed;
That's where I rest my head.
Oh, my bed, my bed, best place in the town.
The town, the town, oh, such a good place,
My bed, my bed, is the best.

Amy Verrill (12)
St Patrick's Catholic College, Thornaby

School Pressure

I stayed up late finishing the work.
I didn't want to get up, didn't want to leave the house.
But, oh, the dread of it sitting unfinished.
Could've gone back to sleep, that's all I actually wanted to do.
I didn't want to wake up, get dressed, get ready.
It was horrible, really.
I didn't want to go, never actually to go,
Just had to, but the school pressure.
I would leave the door, I would walk, then arrive.
Didn't want to leave the bed, didn't want to come back to reality,
But I had to go to school, had to be there,
Never wanted to go, but I had to, the school pressure.

Alex Bryan (12)
St Patrick's Catholic College, Thornaby

My Farfetched Dream

Ever since I was a kid, I've always
wanted to explore. Unlike other kids
my age I was a lot more curious
so when kids decided to be footballers,
or doctors, lawyers, engineers,
I was a bit more different. I want
to pursue a more farfetched
dream. Well, I know it would
be difficult but still I want to
be an astronomical scientist which
not many people even know about
but I will never give up. 'Cause
whatever I set my mind on, I can achieve.

Peniel Agbanyim (13)
St Patrick's Catholic College, Thornaby

Football Fun

As I run on the pitch, you know it's real now.
I tackle the other player easily.
I run to the goal to do a two-step.
Then crowds roar and so do I.
Ready to smash this game
Here it goes, 1-1, but not for long.
I jump in the air and bicycle kick that ball to that goal.
In it goes and so do I.
Fun, you think, more like amazing
And money making
And look at their tackle for the ball.
I just stand back, laugh,
Tackle the ball then off I go.

Elena Dew (12)
St Patrick's Catholic College, Thornaby

Injustice To Blame

I put my heart in this.
Blood, sweat, pain all again.
Constant blame.
Over, over, over, and over again
I want to forget the past
That created this disgraced anger through my veins
Sending me insane
Why, why do I always feel the pain?
I want to forget the fate that put me in this place
My whole family tree riddled with injustice
I want to forget the lot of the past
That pushed me over the edge.

James Hannah (13)
St Patrick's Catholic College, Thornaby

My Love For Animals

A nimals are kind creatures if you treat them right.

N o animal should be treated badly

I love animals because they make me feel calm and relaxed

M y favourite animal is a pig.

A ll animals should be treated with respect, and they will respect you back.

L ovely animals are everywhere

S ome animals can be harsh, but be patient and kind to them.

Sophie Russell (11)

St Patrick's Catholic College, Thornaby

Taking My Bike In The Woods

One day I took my bike into the woods
and it was my first time
so I was excited but nervous at the same time,
I could see many things, including birds,
and the luminous light of my bike light leading the way.
I could hear owls hooting
birds chirping
and the sound of the gravel crunching beneath my tyres.
I enjoy stuff like this
although I don't get to do it often.

Noah Burwood-Conroy (11)
St Patrick's Catholic College, Thornaby

Africa

The rivers, like the clear blue pearls.
The lands, the soils, the animals, forever here blooming
in grace.
The hot, warm air hugging my skin like clouds.
Oh, Africa, how your beauty blooms
Like nothing my eyes have seen.
The languages, as unique as ever.
The blood of every African woman runs in my veins.

Janet David (12)
St Patrick's Catholic College, Thornaby

My Favourite Place On Earth

My room, my favourite place on Earth,
My room, with my comfy bed,
My duvet, it feeds my warmth.
My pillows, wait until you see,
My pillows, soft as can be.
Oh, my room, my stunning clothes,
My shoes, they're worth running for.
My room, oh, my room,
I will stay forever,
My bed, I will lie.

Mia Thompson (12)

St Patrick's Catholic College, Thornaby

Bricks

Brick by brick, society is made.
Dreams are formed.
They are built by us.
We are like mini-figures, built from different legs, torsos and heads.
But still, we are made from the same plastic.
Endless possibilities are built from creativity.
People are bricks, we can connect to make something big or small.

Luke Hill (13)
St Patrick's Catholic College, Thornaby

Things I Like

My name is Theo,
And this is what I like,
Yes, I like fried chicken,
KFC is where I'm sticking,
But I also like football,
Thornaby Town FC is my club,
I'm the captain of the 9,
Which is also very fine,
I believe this is the end,
So thanks for reading,
My friend.

Theo Reed (11)
St Patrick's Catholic College, Thornaby

Two Lives In One

Every day, house to house
The inside world starts to shout
Moving from one to the other
The world starts to stop
But continue on
Then join the fun
Pick up a hobby
To escape reality
But don't tell the other,
'Cause they'll start to shout.

Emily Ions (12)
St Patrick's Catholic College, Thornaby

Home

It wraps me and its inhabitants in warmth,
It shelters me,
It takes care of me.
Four rooms upstairs and three downstairs,
Three cats and three humans,
It's surely not chaotic,
Spare room takes longest to get to;
Black and red car.

Sam Brown (12)
St Patrick's Catholic College, Thornaby

Spain

Oh, Spain
How sunny you are
Bringing a shine into my life
Oh, how great you are
Views on top of views
Amongst the stars
Oh, how shiny you are
Oh, what a fairy tale
Among the midnight sky
I say
Never rainy
Oh, how summery you are
Bringing memories
Never forgotten.

Ava Matthews (12)
St Patrick's Catholic College, Thornaby

Football

Football is like my truth
It keeps me going
It lets me enjoy myself
It relieves me when I am angry
It helps me whenever I kick the ball revealing
Dreaming of me becoming a professional
Feeling the wind blowing on my face.

Cailan Wilberforce (12)
St Patrick's Catholic College, Thornaby

The Things About Me

The things about me are:
My name is Faye
My bed is where I lie
I have one brother
And he is like no other
I have a pet dog
He is brown like a log
I like gymnastics
Because I'm made of elastic.

Faye Horner (11)
St Patrick's Catholic College, Thornaby

I Rock

I play my guitar,
Baptised at an altar,
Coming at you from afar,
That's what I said,
My favourite colour's red,
I want to go to bed,
Instead, I read,
I play my Xbox,
Let's rock,
I go fishing on the dock,
My studio I lock.

Isaac Woodgate (13)
St Patrick's Catholic College, Thornaby

Boro!

I believe
I believe
I believe that football is the one for me
I believe football is the best for me
I believe a footballer is the one to be
I believe
I believe.

Luke Forsyth (13)
St Patrick's Catholic College, Thornaby

Middlesbrough

Boro, my team, my home
Isaiah Jones on the right wing, with him we always win
The tree will always stand tall in Middlesbrough
Even though he's not here.

Sonny Matthews (11)
St Patrick's Catholic College, Thornaby

My Dreams

In my dreams, a ghost was in town,
It had a white dress, was transparent, and its hair was brown.

In my dreams, it was peaceful and sunny,
Birds were chirping and there was a rainbow bunny.

In my dreams, the stove was messy and I was in a cave,
Inside, colour and lasers, it was a rave.

In my dreams, I was in a tree in a park,
Dogs were walking and the only word they said was *bark*.

In my dreams, I was on the Eiffel Tower in France,
I was standing still in a menacing stance.

In my dreams, I never woke up,
For I was in heaven, way up, up, up.

Alexander Martin (11)
St Thomas More High School, Westcliff-On-Sea

The Dueling Purple Dragons

On this day, the night will fall,
Purple duelling dragons will save them all,
Their roars are deafening,
Sending shivers down my spine,
The end of the world will be today,
When they're enlarging every day,
In my eyes, the reflecting of purple fire,
Moving up and ascending to the lord,
The police now will never be bored,
As these demons travel in herds,
I wish to go to sleep tonight,
Hoping to see the sun shine so bright,
The night sky is now in flames,
That are purple like Halloween parades,
This is never to be heard again,
As that night now shall be dead.

Ethan Newson (11)
St Thomas More High School, Westcliff-On-Sea

Life's Prophecy

War and poverty,
People taking others' property.
This is not life's prophecy.
Being unique is good for you.
Don't be an imitation, don't pick or choose.
The world has changed,
And it's definitely strange.
People invading others' homes,
We need to have some shame.

Please have pity,
Some people are not so lucky,
You have a roof above your head,
Others do not have money,
So try to donate to charity,
Live out our prophecy.

Zane Noubayo (11)
St Thomas More High School, Westcliff-On-Sea

The Changing Wind

A boy full of grin,
Said hello to the lovely wind.
Wind startled, gets ready to push,
Until a nearby bush flew and went *whoosh*.
The boy, scared, is unaware,
He is being chased by a bear.
And maybe a table too,

He is running for his life,
Till he finds some tiny mice.
He thought they were cute,
Until he got slapped with a shoe.
This was all a dream,
Yet he still felt the wind.

Kristupas Margenis (11)
St Thomas More High School, Westcliff-On-Sea

Dreams

I've always wanted to be rich,
But it only happens in my dreams.
I want to help the poor,
But it's only possible in my dreams.
Every single day, I want people to like each other more,
But it's only possible in my dreams.
I want all the people in the world to be happy,
But that only happens in my dreams,
But it can become a reality,
Only if people are kind.

Ogie Odigie (11)
St Thomas More High School, Westcliff-On-Sea

Are You Ready?

Happy or sad?
Lonely or guilty?
Never had friends, looking for motivation,
want to be powerful,
want to be excited,
stuff that haunts you,
stuff you don't like,
now you never give up,
the battle ahead,
the battle of life.

Somtochukwu Ofomata-Aghaenu (11)
St Thomas More High School, Westcliff-On-Sea

The Lands End

L ovely view
A tlantic ocean
N othing but water
D elicious fish and chips
S and-filled beaches

E nd of land
N ever-ending grass
D unes of sand fill the land.

Kacper Nawrocki (11)
St Thomas More High School, Westcliff-On-Sea

In Another Universe

In another universe,
Maybe we could live free,
Without a care in the world,
Just us, like we agreed.

Maybe in another universe,
You wouldn't have to see me cry.
I would be happy and joyful,
Make life seem worthwhile.

Possibly in another universe,
I could love with no regrets.
I might hate who I am,
But I'd like to forget.

What about in another universe,
Where I'd done everything right.
I could be there for you,
No matter the time.

If I start to think about it,
Maybe just for once,
It's always in another universe,
Why can't it just be this one?

Acacia Carys Bisssue (15)
The Duston School, Duston

134

All About Patsy (Football)

P lays football for Kingsthorpe Jets Raptors U12, but I might be leaving soon - fresh start is good, isn't it?

A bracadabra... I can't just make goals appear in the blink of an eye, I have to work too, you know - my team knows that, don't they?

T he coaches like to shout... it just makes me better, doesn't it?

S triker in football but also can play centre-back, not a goalkeeper! Different positions make me better, don't they?

Y es, I have been on the team for a year and a bit, but I'm already being replaced by someone who has just played a week - but unfairness makes me a better person, doesn't it?

Patsy Nutt (12)
The Duston School, Duston

The Beautiful Truth Is

The beautiful truth is,
How are we meant to know our identity,
Or that we have to change
When our brains are fully developed,
And yet we're already having to follow what we get told.
How do we know what it is we want
If we're doing what they tell us,
How do we know how to live freely
If we've been trapped in four walls,
Not knowing what we want ourselves.

Nathaniel Harris (14)
The Duston School, Duston

Sports

Sports, some the same, some different,
They all get played differently,
And they all have different rules, so listen,
Bat and ball, hit the ball, cricket, baseball,
Ball and racket, smash, tennis, table tennis,
Foot and ball, goal,
Football, where legends are made.
Bullets and gun, bang, shooting,
All of these sports are professional
And all of them are different.

Jake Kitching (12)
The Duston School, Duston

Is S/He Okay?

As I walk down the street, I see a man asleep on the floor, I wonder, is he okay?
As I walk with my friend, I think, is he okay?
As I walk past a coffee shop I see a man sitting alone with his dog and I wonder, is he okay?
As I sit alone in my living room, I wonder, am I okay?

Always think about others, but never forget yourself.

James Moore (15)
The Duston School, Duston

Untitled

Lots of teachers can't say my name properly,
Some call me Ishmail,
Like, where do they get the h?
Some call me Ismarle,
Which is what my sister calls me,
Some call me Izmail,
Which I'm fine with,
Honestly, I don't care what you call me,
Just don't call me I Smile or Ice Spice!

Ismail Njie (12)
The Duston School, Duston

Change

Change needs to happen in the world.
War needs to stop and peace needs to be accepted.
War is destroying our world and making it more dangerous.
If war stopped we could improve and make the world a
better place instead of destroying it.
But all we need is a little bit of change.

Mason Phillips (12)

The Duston School, Duston

140

Friends

F riends are important
R ely on friends, they can help you
I ndependence is not always key
E veryone needs a friend
N ever be mean
D on't be rude to your friends.

Coleton Vickery (11)

The Duston School, Duston

The World

The world is like your emotions.
Sometimes you're happy,
Sometimes you're not.
Maybe sometimes it's raining,
Sometimes it's sunny,
But the world lives within you,
So embrace it.

Mark Aning (14)
The Duston School, Duston

My Life (Literally!)

The time I felt truly free,
Was the time my mind collapsed completely.
It's Friday; some people say it's their favourite day,
Not for me, for a great deal of reasons
Like my mum won't stop nagging about the really small things.
As small as 'make your bed' turns into the most heated argument ever. Sometimes I realise there's something wrong,
But I don't know what. Is it me? Am I not perfect?
That's what I think, not compared to my sister.
Sometimes I start the fight but I can't always get out of it.
It's like I'm angry, anxious and argumentative all at the same time.
I even make my parents cry and go mad at times,
Like, what is wrong with me? I start feeling dizzy.
In the back of my mind, I hear my parents shouting at me.
"Get out!" I scream loudly, but really,
I'm sure everyone's thinking,
Should I jump out the window...
No, that's too much.

Riley Davies (13)
The Excelsior Academy, London

143

Who I Am

I'm a boy with short black hair,
I'm a boy who likes to be fair with everyone.

I'm a boy who was born in Italy.
But when I was 2 years old, I had to leave tearfully.
Then I came to the UK.
I was a little bit sad, but now I'm okay.

I'm a boy who likes to play football,
I eagerly wait for the ball,
But then I remember I have asthma,
So then I take the position of the keeper,
And make incredible saves.
I hope to be a keeper in many more games.

I'm a boy who likes to read the Quran
And learn the teachings of Prophet Muhammad to act on,
And that is how goodness spreads.

I'm a boy who spends time with his mum and dad,
And this makes me very glad,
Knowing that they are always by my side,
I am the boy.

Tanzil Hossain (11)
The Excelsior Academy, London

Poetry Is Truth

Poetry is truth
The possibilities on what to write are endless
Poetry is truth
However or whatever you write is a form of art, it's poetry
Poetry is truth
Write about what you love and hate about anything
Poetry is truth
Always know you have great potential to make amazing
poetry
Step into the world of a specific and unique thing: Poetry!
Whatever poem you read, it will always be inspiring
Or it can be funny
The choice is yours to make
Wherever you are
Whoever you are, you know
Poetry is truth
Any time or every time you want to
You can write a poem
But remember
Poetry is truth.

Laura Krysa (13)
The Excelsior Academy, London

Football

F ootball, a game that fills people with such adrenaline.

O f course, there's a debate; who's better, Messi or CR7?

O bviously, Messi has more Ballon d'Ors and has more

T rophies, but Ronaldo has performed in more leagues and has match

B alls and golden boots. He is also such an

A erial threat, which makes him such a danger. Also, there's

L ewandowski, who scored five goals in nine minutes. Incredible!

L uis Suárez is amazing too, football is amazing!

Ty Osman (13)
The Excelsior Academy, London

Social Media

Social media, social media is fake,
Unrealistic expectations.
Everyone is beautiful,
No matter the blemishes.
Lots of people feel concerned,
About how they look on social media.
This needs to stop completely.
I feel angry.

Why does everyone care so much,
About how they look?
Some people Photoshop their pictures.
You're beautiful no matter what.
People don't feel confident,
We need to change that.

Ela'Rose Tumburi (12)
The Excelsior Academy, London

147

A Human's True Colours

It's weird that we have to fit in the standards
But hey, why don't we embrace our impurities
Because life is short
So live it how you want.

But you say who cares?
What's life if we have to do what we don't want to do
And yes, it may hurt
And insecurities are the worst.
Don't let others drag you down.

Love everything about you
Before you ask why you didn't
Live life how you wanted to.

Aisha Abdulle (11)
The Excelsior Academy, London

Real? Fake? Lie? Truth?

Fearing the bad spirits surrounding,
Abandoned within the lying,
Knowledge rejecting the way I am feeling,
Eager to search for the relation,
Why is it me that symbolises this confusion?
Oh, the conflict injects into my beliefs,
Revealing.

Sofiat Bankole (12)
The Excelsior Academy, London

Funerals

I never thought I would say goodbye,
Now I stand before you with tears in my eye.
Now we lay your soul to rest,
Maybe it's for the best.
The white roses I lay before you,
Show how pure you were.
The overwhelming grief of losing someone special,
The speeches told by our family's generation
Portray the loss of our dearest.

Rebecca Praisey (17)

The Mews School, Wem

The Secret Recipe

Get yourself prepared with aprons and dressings,
Get those ingredients, it's great for the lesson.
Get them bowls, put them in and stir it around,
Get the mixer and mix until it is brown.

Add a tablespoon of baking soda and stir it in,
If you forget, then put it in the bin,
Add a tablespoon of vanilla and make sure to stir,
If you forget, then put it in the bin.

Get it in the oven and set it to seven,
Get yourself a timer and set it to eleven.
Add a bit of dressing like sprinkles for your sake,
If you did it right, you'll have yourself a cake!

Alex Holloway (12)
The Salesian Academy Of St John Bosco, Bootle

Living Under Another Student's Light

In this poem, I'll write my soul away,
And at my best, I'll give all I have to say.
My life is about being another student's shadow.

Seated in a classroom with my tiresome pen,
Words written on my page, no more than ten,
The clock ticks alongside every heartbeat my soul gives.

Thud, thud, thud,
Cries my heart with intent.
Will nobody hear my cry for help?
Is nobody able to tell?

My brain is constantly clouded with thoughts,
From which, "I'm not good enough," exclaims without
knowing pause.
Negative whispers fill my ears,
Each imploring me to give up my hard work.
And again, my life is about being another student's shadow.

From my science textbook
To my English annotations.
A group of jumbled-up incoherences,
To which my brain scatters into pieces.
I'm suffocated by my own high standards.
Engulfed by life's playing cards as I dance helplessly
On life's thin line.

I'm only sixteen, I'm just a kid,
With a whole life to live.
A working life, of suffering and pain,
Probably for someone else's gain.
My life will always be about being another student's shadow.

I want to be smart, I want to be enough.
I want to be known for doing great things.

But the stress I'm currently undergoing,
Makes me seem that I'm not fit.

Princess Adora Aiyeki Uyinmwen (16)
The Salesian Academy Of St John Bosco, Bootle

War Will Never Change

War will never change,
Just as the number of lives it has taken.
War will never change,
Just as arguing against it will always be forsaken.

To fight in a war doesn't take away from the murders done,
Some people thinking of war as only child's play and fun.
To hate war, is to hate anguish and death,
Soldiers only being remembered through a cold trembling breath.

War will never change,
For those who have been affected by it.
War will never change,
Just as the amount of problems it has caused.

War will never change.

Caiden Molloy (14)
The Salesian Academy Of St John Bosco, Bootle

I Quit

I quit trying to make bad people happy
I quit putting bad people before my family
I know it's my fault I'm quitting
But it's for my own good
These bad people make me do bad stuff
I just quit
I want the best for the future
I quit...
Knife crime is bad
I don't want it for the future families
I just quit like you should too
So if you see any crime
Just report it to the police
It will make the world better
So don't join gangs
It will ruin your mental health
So stay with your family
And stay away from crime
So you'll be safe all the time.

Lucas Bradbury (13)
The Salesian Academy Of St John Bosco, Bootle

Truth Of Young Kids' Feelings

Work after work, day after day
More homework every day
More pressure on our minds
Our future is key
But not with this type of pressure
We can't have fun
We have no time
Our mind is key
We spend seven hours a day in school
Thirty-five hours per week
The pressure grows as we go up in years
Year seven, year eight, year nine, exams, exams
We choose our choices for exams next year
We'll have to study every day to do well
We try to make our parents proud
We are the future.

Mylie Walsh (12)
The Salesian Academy Of St John Bosco, Bootle

Home Life

Day after day,
Night after night,
My home is where I lay,
But outside is my light,
My home is where I work,
Tired and exhausted,
But it's where my parents smirk,
This all seems normal,
Working non-stop,
When actually it's awful,
Working until my hands throb,
This is very toxic,
But not to me,
I am used to this stuff,
But that shouldn't be,
This is known as child labour,
You may struggle to tell someone,
Even if it's your close neighbour.

Mya Albert-Standley (12)
The Salesian Academy Of St John Bosco, Bootle

Hello?

Hello, hello
Where are you?
Hello?
I am all alone
I need help

Hi
Hello
Hi, where are you?
Everywhere
I am God

God?
Yes my child
Help me
I will set your vision free
From the sins

Now I can see
The colourful flowers
The blue sky
The wildlife
I live and die.

Joseph Johnson (12)
The Salesian Academy Of St John Bosco, Bootle

Alone

There is comfort in being alone
Especially with the safety of home
With a nice cup of tea
Just my thoughts and me
Yes, there are comforts in being alone

In the dark, I hide my fear
All alone my fears come to life
Outside I'm smiling
Inside I'm crying.

Elba Ludovic (13)
The Salesian Academy Of St John Bosco, Bootle

The Forest

In the trees, the leaves move every day,
And the animal in it is having lots of fun,
But somehow, there is no pun,
The animals are having a bad time, though,
If you did see them, it would very much show,
Because of what happened a long time ago.

Niall Hiddleston (12)
The Salesian Academy Of St John Bosco, Bootle

Money Is The Reason

Money,
Money makes us happy,
Well, that's what they say,
Money is bad really,
At the end of the day,
It buys us nice clothes and shoes,
But then why is money so bad?
I think it's great,
It feels cold,
It makes me smile,
When I use my money,
I don't cry.

Chloe Williams (13)
The Salesian Academy Of St John Bosco, Bootle

Beauty Exists

Beauty exists all around the world.
Everyone is perfect the way they are.
We are all different in our own ways.
Everyone is perfect the way they are.
Everyone is unique.
No matter what anyone says,
You're perfect in your own way.

Marie Didiova (13)
The Salesian Academy Of St John Bosco, Bootle

Hobbies

As I think
Hobby is happy
If you have a hobby
You are so happy.
So many hobbies:
Playing, reading, cooking,
Playing, reading, cooking,
If you have a hobby
You will be happy...

Thisarani Satharasinghage (13)
The Salesian Academy Of St John Bosco, Bootle

Dance

I go to dance every few days,
And I love it,
I have a ton of friends there,
And whenever I go to dance, I feel like I belong there,
It makes me really happy when I start dancing.

Olivia Reeves (12)
The Salesian Academy Of St John Bosco, Bootle

Salt And Pepper Chicken

Who doesn't love salt and pepper chicken?
The perfection of it
It is juicy and succulent
If you don't like it
Try fried chicken, or buttermilk chicken.

Brandon Forsyth (12)
The Salesian Academy Of St John Bosco, Bootle

I Don't Like School

I don't like school, no siree
Not maths, not English, or history
School isn't fun
I'd rather go run
The work, the work
All the homework.

Ranveer Singh-Korwajz (13)
The Salesian Academy Of St John Bosco, Bootle

Untitled

Every war, millions are killed.
Hearts are the opposite of filled.
All their families sitting at home
Find out forever they will be alone.

Sophie Hanlon (12)
The Salesian Academy Of St John Bosco, Bootle

Life Is Like A Disney Channel Movie

How fragile can a heart be?
After that day, it's never been the same.
I tried to give the million pieces she broke.
Back into the fire she started.
My mind held onto those words she said,
Now I know that the note was foolish.
I should've been better and more confident,
Better like him.
I can't look at her the same,
You were my fire, my heart and soul.
I guess what they say is true,
Love really is a game,
A game you just can't win.
I dreamed of getting married
And starting a family,
But what is it that he has that I don't?
Is he stronger?
Is he more funny?
Is he more pretty than me?
But out of all the people you know
Why my best friend?
Now, I'm sorry if I tear up,
But I just wanted to ask,
How fragile can a heart be?

Gabriel Pinto (14)
The Thetford Academy, Thetford

A Guide For The Lost

Earlier this morning, I was struggling.
My friend was trying to understand,
How true love was difficult to fathom.
And it got me thinking,
True love, shouldn't be this complicated,
I thought I would understand by now.
No hard feelings, but these feelings are hard to decipher.
Only person on the street with a door people can knock on,
I want to help others with this, I should put a light on.
This is dedicated to you if you've
Felt the lowest of the low,
I know how you feel, you don't want to struggle anymore.
I used to fall hard, now I don't even bother anymore.
Maybe we wipe away the tears,
Turn around and face our fears.
Maybe we all need a guide to take us
Out of the eye of the storm.
We all need a way to escape,
To flourish.

Theodore Higgins (14)
The Thetford Academy, Thetford

I Love, Like And Hate

I love the feeling of winning that one match,
I like the feeling of that one-handed catch,
I hate the feeling of always being cold,
I love the feeling of being young, not old,
I like the feeling of waking up in the sun,
I hate the feeling when school is never fun,
I love the feeling when I see my favourite thing to eat,
I like the feeling of when Man U is never beat,
I hate the feeling of a really messy room,
I love listening to my favourite tune,
I like the feeling of getting a good night's rest,
I hate the feeling of not being able to do my best,
I love the feeling of dribbling past a player,
I like the feeling when there's no work to do later,
I hate the feeling of my hair in a bun,
I love the feeling of knowing there's much more to come.

Lola Fowler (12)
The Thetford Academy, Thetford

Boys Have Emotions

Boys have emotions.
Boys and men shouldn't hide their emotions just for them to look brave or be a knight in shining armour.
Men and boys are brave and knights in shining armour while expressing and showing feelings.
I would rather have boys crying and showing emotion than have one thinking they can't show emotion.
So boys, when you show emotions, be brave, be strong about it.
Don't let people tell you you're not brave for showing emotion, just brush them off your shoulder.
Be brave showing your emotion.
Be unstoppable showing your emotion.
Learn how to love yourself by being you
And not hiding any emotion, let it all out.

Chloeanne Newell (14)
The Thetford Academy, Thetford

How Much I Have

I am made of moments that bring me down
Moments that may present a frown
But with all I've been through, happy and sad
Makes me think of how much I have

It all went by so very quick
But when you think of it, it gives you a kick
So when you have good moments, you think of the bad
And it make me think of how much I have

For I have family who love me and friends who care
Which I'm given to understand is quite rare
And I have now decided that it's fair to say
It makes me think of how much I have today.

Buddie Hogg (13)
The Thetford Academy, Thetford

I Don't Know What To Write...

I don't know what to write
My paper is empty, dull and white
Not a single thought in my mind
Not a single thought for me to find
The clock is slowly ticking away
My mind is driving me away

This poem isn't very deep
I'd rather be at home asleep
The clock continues to tick, I'm wary
My words truly do not vary
Once I've finished this, it will be night, because
I don't know what to write.

Cian Finch (13)
The Thetford Academy, Thetford

Different

I believe that everyone is different in their own way,
Not everyone looks the same.
You might like other things,
It is your choice, not someone else's.
Different,
I believe that everyone is not the same,
Some people might be twins but still have different tastes,
Some people might like dogs over cats.
Don't try to be like everyone else,
Be different.

Ornela Raudonyte (12)
The Thetford Academy, Thetford

Dog Haiku

Dogs are very cool.
I believe they are the best,
For they are so cute.

Youssef Bedair (12)
Therfield School, Leatherhead

In The Dance I Will

Motivation is the spark that lights a way,
A fleeting flame that beckons us to play.
In whispers, dreams of mountains we could climb,
A burst of passion that ignores the time.

But discipline, it's steady as the tide,
The constant push that keeps us on the ride.
It wakes us up when motivation sleeps,
And holds our hands through valleys, dark and deep.

For dreams are built on moments, day by day,
Not just on fire, but bricks we set in clay.
So let them dance together hand in hand,
Motivation sparks, discipline will stand.

Ethan Hogan (16)
Thomas Becket Catholic School, Northampton

Autumn

The crunchy leaves
And crisp air
The wind blowing
Through your hair
Conkers cracking open as they drop
Ducks splash as they plop
Warm cosy evenings by the fire
The flame getting higher and higher
Low sun at night
Making the leaves look golden and bright
Blowing cobwebs in the wind
Hear the birds swoop and sing
Autumn is near
If you see and hear these things appear
When it does know it's close
To the best time of the year.

Olivia-Mae Overton-Arch (13)

Thomas Becket Catholic School, Northampton

Bee-Zzz Happy

I got stung by a bee-zzz
It was hurting painfully-zzz
I got rushed to the A&E-zzz
People were worried-zzz
But I am now a happy bee-zzz
I still can't play footie-zzz
So I'm getting angry-zzz
Because my injuries-zzz
Won't be making a recovery-zzz.

Eduard Mateescu (13)

Thomas Becket Catholic School, Northampton

True Beauty

Beauty is just like an attractive book cover.
Beauty is just like a wonderful friendship.
In every friendship you will always be beautiful.
Beauty is about what is on the inside, not the outside.
Always be happy about your beauty.
Don't care about what other people think of you.
Care about what you think of yourself.
Like me. I always thought I was ugly.
But once I saw the other side of me, I saw I was beautiful.
No matter what others think of me.
I have good, beautiful and nice encouraging friends.
No matter their opinion I always followed my heart.
So should you.
There are different types of beauty.
E.g. everlasting beauty, natural beauty, artificial beauty and made-up beauty.
Which one do you think you have?

IniOluwa Akanbi (11)
Thornaby Academy, Thornaby

179

The Goodness In Animals' Inner Personality

Lost and timid by the predators
Aren't predators us humans?
Dragging animals and sending them demands
Crying for help that is far away
We become greedy day by day
Some animals are peaceful and pleasant
A bunny as pure as white silk
As light as a feather
As gentle as smooth skin
Aren't predators us human?
Harming and destroying the wildlife
Opening our sharp knives
A dark smoke infecting our hearts with evil
Surrendering ourselves for money
Sacrificing animals for benefits
Controlling them bit by bit
Consuming them with monstrosity
Aren't predators us humans?
Filled with nothing but greed
Aren't predators us humans?

Daniella Abioye (12)
Thornaby Academy, Thornaby

Beauty Of Nature

Below, a sea of a clear blue sky,
Trees emerge, and mountains rise,
Along with bonsai,
The puffy clouds dance in the air,
Abundant grass munched by hare,
A wave of delight fills the space,
Wonders and ponders along with grace.
Bold strokes of brown and green,
Beautiful nature, yet few people so keen,
A world where man and nature merge,
Awe and wonder emerge,
In the vast ocean of pure blue.

The deer wild and world limpid,
We connect both with art,
The vision of mankind along with nature ever so clear,
Art giving passion, art giving nature a chance.

Daniel Abioye (13)
Thornaby Academy, Thornaby

Life Is ABout Ups And Downs

Life has different stages,
Even when it turns to crumbs.
But there's one phrase,
Which goes like:
"It don't matter what is happening,
Don't lose your hope no matter what!"
This world has different paths
Sometimes we go in the sky
And sometimes we go in the mud.
But no matter what
We should be happy.
The thing I care about is mental health.
This is because if you don't care about your health,
Life will be a large rock in front of you.
The only way the rock will crumble is if
You care about your health.

Noor Zafar (11)
Thornaby Academy, Thornaby

Never Give Up

The time I feel free is when I have a football by my feet on an empty pitch.

At one point, I wanted to give up on football because I wasn't really that good.

Until I said to myself, *I wasn't raised to be a quitter.*

And I kept going, and I got better and better each day.

I believe that if I can do it, anybody can do it.

The only way you will ever improve on football is if you train.

You will not be better than you were before if you don't try to be.

You will need to train every time you get the chance.

And you will make your dreams come true.

Alfie Wing (13)
Thornaby Academy, Thornaby

Forgot

How did I forget?
How, how, how?
How did I forget
How to be me?

What do you say when you're feeling blue?
Nobody knows, nobody knows

Mum, please help me, I'm drowning in my own tears
Mum, I think there's something wrong with me
Take me to the doctors ASAP
She says I'm fine, but I don't feel fine
How did I forget, how, how, how?

I forgot, I forgot
How to be me

Sometimes I just want to cry, but then it's too painful for me
to cry
F-o-r-g-o-t.

Evelyn Brown (12)
Vale Of York Academy, Clifton Without

Pollution

P oor animals get stuck in your thrown-away rubbish.

O cean, what a lovely place, until you see all the waste underneath.

L evels of the sea are rising.

L evels of CO_2 are rising.

U nder the water that you use as a bin,

T he creatures are hating, they want to be free.

I ntoxicated chemicals are killing the animals.

O cean, what a lovely place, but only from above.

N ow is the time for change.

Natalia Szajczyk (13)
Vale Of York Academy, Clifton Without

185

The Sound Of Sport

The swoop of my racket
by my head
The spring of the shuttlecock
going over the net
The squeak of shoes
across the court

The bash of the ball
going into the net
The yelling of the players
towards the ref
The words they yell
'foul', 'pen'

The sound of sport
is what I hear
The sound of sport
is when everyone cheers.

Lennon Fergie (11)
Vale Of York Academy, Clifton Without

Pizza

I like baking
I like cooking
Cooking pizza, yes, with that topping
Cheese and sauce, but don't forget the olives
Then give me some pepperoni, because I'm cooking
Cooking for a feast, for all my friends, yeah
Cheese and sauce, but don't forget the olives
Then give me some pepperoni, make me more because I'm
going on tour
So please don't bore, and make some more
If it is bad I will be sad
So let's cook, so I won't be mad
Add extra sauce, yes, I will enforce
If you don't give enough, I will throw ham and then it will go
bang.

Jamie Siviter (12)
Whitchurch High School, Cardiff

Cats

There are lots of different cats.
There are fat cats, skinny cats,
Lots of cats.
Sometimes a cat can be good at hunting and some are not.
Some cats think they're pretty,
While others don't think they are.
There are different types of cats, lions, tigers, etc,
They're all different on the outside,
But they might be the same on the inside.
They might look big and scary but are nice,
Or they might deceive you with
Their nice looks and be the complete opposite.
The point is,
Be whatever cat you want to be.
The choice is yours.

Dalia Tarik (12)
Whitchurch High School, Cardiff

Weather

S torm is a beast
T ook your happiness
O ut of calm
R ain is a song with sadness to
M elt your heart

R ain is a witch
A ttacking your heart
I ce to freeze your heart with
N o more love

F loods are horrible
L et you cry with
O ut of calm
O ut of wine
D ot your life.

Adan Chan (12)
Whitchurch High School, Cardiff

Slinky

S wimming
L ove hearts
I ce
N o school
K atie
Y ellow.

Josie Jeffreys (13)
Whitchurch High School, Cardiff

How Do You Know?

How do you know it's real
When I'm smiling ear to ear?
How do you know it's not fake
And I'm holding back the tears?
How do you know?
Before you judge that I'm facing battles of my own
How do you know how far I'd go to protect my friends?
How do you know that when I'm sad
I don't want to be a burden?
How do you know I'm not lying when I say I'm fine?
How do you know when I really want to lock myself away
and cry?
How do you know that I'm slowly fading away?
How do you know that I'm struggling every single day?
Yeah, I guess I'm okay,
If 'O' stands for overwhelmed by my surroundings
If 'K' stands for kicking the wall until my leg is pounding
If 'A' stands for asking myself if I'm enough
And 'Y' stands for 'Why do I have to act tough?'
How do you know when I say I'm fine, that I'm not lying
And just don't want to let you inside?

Lexie Black (13)
Wollaston School, Wollaston

A Dream

A dream is a place to wander,
A dream is a place to roam.
But not all who wander,
Have to wander alone.

Be there for someone,
And they'll be there for you.
Your life might light up like the sun,
With them stood alongside you.

Don't copy yourself from a bunch of lies,
Set your imagination free.
Live a thousand lifetimes,
And be everything you want to be.

So listen to words of wisdom,
And let them be a guide.
But set yourself apart from them,
You can battle your own fight.

And take a quick step back,
To look at what you've been.
All those things that you have done,
Yet there's so much more to be seen.

You'll make some of your greatest memories,
With a friend by your side.
And without them your life might have more worries,
You may need a friend from time to time.

So head off back to bed,
But not for too much more.
Be excited for the day ahead,
And what you can explore.

A dream is a place to wander,
A dream is a place to roam.
But if you think about it,
A dream is rubbish alone.

Oliver Goodes (12)
Wollaston School, Wollaston

The Candour Behind The Chords

One night I'm sitting, just sitting.
Finding a place where I'm fitting.
Putting on music and finding a place to relax.
Or escaping to a world of country or folk, rock or blues,
The world where the truth will out in your mind.

If you dig deep enough you might find the candour behind
the chords, or the truth behind your favourite tunes.
Maybe you like metal, or listening to angry baboons, they all
have meaning.
Johnny Cash seems to like chickens and love, while Madness
has the wings of a dove.
Not all songs are like that, though The Specials didn't lack
that.
'Free Nelson Mandela' speaks for itself.
Knowing it was cruel to lock him up for twenty-seven years,
imagine the tears!

They let him out once aware of his innocence.
Inspired by their vigilance?
This really does prove, the candour behind the chords.

Liam Barras (13)
Wollaston School, Wollaston

But

When things get rough, you may want to quit
Words may fill you, like 'I'm not good enough, that's it.'
You may want to slump and sit

I like animals
But people are allergic
I think quadrobics is the best sport
But people disagree
I was born in England
But others were born all around the world
I love Halloween
But my family doesn't celebrate it
I like making masks
But others called me weird
I am me, as funny, caring and as weird as they come!
And others, this time, they can't disagree.

Juliana Pollock (11)
Wollaston School, Wollaston

The Unwanted Guest

Autumn is my favourite season
But there is one thing I detest
It's not the wind, the rain, the dark
It's the unwanted guest.

He creeps across the floors
Along the skirting boards
He walks up the walls
Then scurries through the doors.

He occupies the corners
He makes himself at home
With tiny eyes and hairy legs
He's free to spin, sail and roam.

I wish that I was braver
And could ask him to leave
But we've learnt to live together
And I call my spider, Steve.

Elizabeth O'Keeffe (11)
Wollaston School, Wollaston

Never Judge A Mango By Its Skin

The first time I ate a mango,
It was amazing,
So let me present to you what type of mangos you may find.

Some mangos can be squishy.
Some can be rough,
Some can be small,
Some can be big,
Some can be juicy,
Some can be dry.

Yet, no mango deserves to be thrown away,
Because they may not look perfect, juicy or big,
So next time you find a mango that doesn't look right,
Don't throw it away. Try it.
You never know it may be nice.

Zachary Odell (12)
Wollaston School, Wollaston

Hugo The French Bulldog

Hugo is a bulldog, small and stout,
with a wrinkly face and a little snout.
He loves to play and run around,
chasing his tail, he spins on the ground.
Hugo loves treats, he'll beg and plead
for a tasty snack he'll always need.
He's my best friend, loyal and true.
We go on walks, he struts with pride,
with his tiny legs he's by my side.
Hugo the bulldog, my funny friend,
life with him is simply great!

Alex Bond (13)
Wollaston School, Wollaston

Behind The Blondie

It may be the girl you called "horse hair"
The girl you shamed for having hay hair
The girl who cries a lot
No, behind that blondie
Is a kind-hearted person
The girl who would kill for her friends
The girl who looks after her five younger brothers
The girl by your side
Always checking on you
Yeah, that's right, you can't face the truth
So that's what's behind the Blondie.

Elisa White (12)
Wollaston School, Wollaston

Failing Before Victory

Winning, losing
Trying, failing
Working, building,
is what makes the best performance in the end.
Winning is not winning without losing first.

Catherine Fairley (12)
Wollaston School, Wollaston

Who Am I?

Who am I?
I am all the writers that I have read
I am all the highlighted lines in the books that speak to me
I am all the people that I have met, all the people I have loved
I am nothing but a mosaic of society
I am like a notebook full of different handwriting, pages worn, corners bent, ink uneven
Yes, I am a daughter and a friend and a writer
Yes, I like singing and music and movies
Yes, I have a mother and friends and blue eyes
But I don't know who I am
I'd say true uniqueness doesn't exist
I am a stained-glass window of all I have learned, everything I've achieved
and everything I will be
But who am I?

Rhianna Lock (17)
Xaverian College, Manchester

Victimised Venture

Victim of my adolescence
Pressurised goal to make new friends
Comments of a clueless mind
Leaving the juvenile strifes behind
New setting to adapt
An upgraded habitat
Perilous pursuit on treacherous desires
I give up, I'm too tired

Victim of my knowledge
Triggering its potential in college
Dedication is surely tested
Every wrong move corrected
Forming doubts of my wisdom
Listening to rules of this kingdom
Just one step closer to freedom

Victim of the truth
It's either I win or I lose
No more games, this is real
To come out on top was the deal
Swallowed by the devastation of reality
Escaping the imprisoning fantasy

Victim of my dream
Law, law, law is calling me
Justification behind the defendant's actions
Their fate sealed by my provocations
The power, the control, the cheers
The dream of many years
The finalised treasure
My victimised venture.

Michelle Rufus (16)
Xaverian College, Manchester

Curious

I am artistic and beautiful.
I am curious about the wonders of the world.
I am the swoosh from the trees, the boom from a firework.
I am diving off the Eiffel Tower into a pot of gold.
I am swimming with the mermaids in the Atlantic.
I am spiders crawling across cobwebs.
I am Michael B Jordan on one knee proposing somewhere in the Caribbean.
I am curious, very curious, who are you?

Amelia Lee (17)
Xaverian College, Manchester

YOUNG WRITERS INFORMATION

We hope you have enjoyed reading this book – and that you will continue to in the coming years.

If you're the parent or family member of an enthusiastic poet or story writer, do visit our website **www.youngwriters.co.uk/subscribe** and sign up to receive news, competitions, writing challenges and tips, activities and much, much more! There's lots to keep budding writers motivated!

If you would like to order further copies of this book, or any of our other titles, then please give us a call or order via your online account.

Young Writers
Remus House
Coltsfoot Drive
Peterborough
PE2 9BF
(01733) 890066
info@youngwriters.co.uk

**Join in the conversation!
Tips, news, giveaways and much more!**

❶ YoungWritersUK   ✖ YoungWritersCW

⦿ youngwriterscw   ♪ youngwriterscw